BEAN DOG
and
NUGGET

The Cookie

Charise Mericle Harper

Alfred A. Knopf

THIS IS A BORZOI BOOK PUBLISHED BY ALFRED A. KNOPF

Visit us on the Web! randomhouse.com/kids
Educators and librarians, for a variety of teaching tools, visit us at RHTeachersLibrarians.com
Library of Congress Cataloging-in-Publication Data
Harper, Charise Mericle.
Bean Dog and Nugget : the cookie / Charise Mericle Harper. — 1st ed.
 p. cm.— (Bean Dog and Nugget)
Summary: Bean Dog and Nugget argue about who will get the bigger half
of a cookie. They try to outwit each other by all sorts of imaginative
means—but they find out that what really counts in the end is friendship.
ISBN 978-0-307-97710-6 (pbk.) — ISBN 978-0-307-97711-3 (lib. bdg.) — ISBN 978-0-307-97712-0 (ebook)
1. Graphic novels. [1. Graphic novels. 2. Sharing—Fiction.
3. Friendship—Fiction. 4. Humorous stories.] I. Title.
PZ7.7.H37Bef 2013
2012029374

The text of this book is set in 16-point Matt Md Text.
The illustrations were created using digital coloring.

MANUFACTURED IN MALAYSIA
May 2013   10 9 8 7 6 5 4 3 2 1   First Edition

Random House Children's Books supports the
First Amendment and celebrates the right to read.

For Luther and Henry,
two boys who like cookies

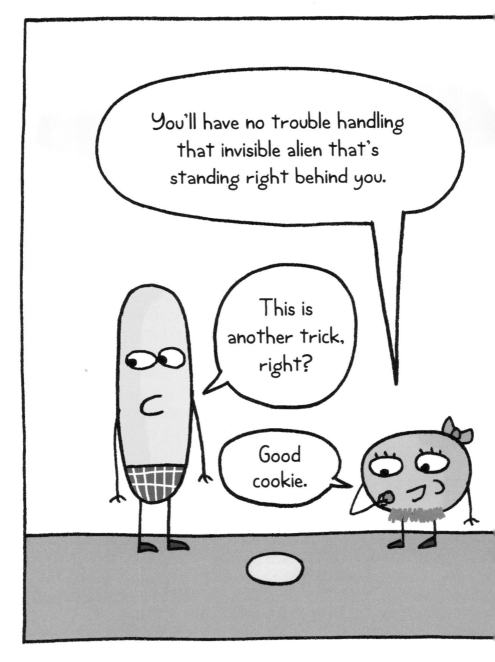